Promise you won't be Cross

Titles in the Bunch:

Clumsy Clumps and the Baby Moon
Millie's Party ~ Monster Eyeballs ~ Happy Sad
Baby Bear Comes Home ~ Peg ~
Big Dog and Little Dog Visit the Moon
Delilah Digs for Treasure ~ Dilly and the Goody-Goody
Horse in the House ~ I Don't Want to Say Yes!
Juggling with Jeremy ~ Keeping Secrets
Mabel and Max ~ Magnificent Mummies
Midnight at Memphis ~ Mouse Flute ~
The Nut Map ~ Owl in the House
Riff-Raff Rabbit ~ Rosie and the Robbers
~ Runaway Fred ~ Tom's Hats
Promise You Won't Be Cross

First published in Great Britain 1999 by Mammoth
an imprint of Egmont Children's Books Limited
239 Kensington High Street, London, W8 6SA
Published in hardback by Heinemann Library,
a division of Reed Educational and Professional Publishing Limited
by arrangement with Egmont Children's Books Limited.

Text copyright © Bel Mooney 1999
Illustrations © Margaret Chamberlain 1999
The Author and Illustrator have asserted their moral rights.
Paperback ISBN 0 7497 3747 6
Hardback ISBN 0 434 80469 X
10 9 8 7 6 5 4 3 2 1
A CIP catalogue record for this title is available from the British Library.
Printed at Oriental Press Limited, Dubai.

Bel Mooney

Promise you won't be Cross

Illustrated by

Margaret Chamberlain

Blue Bananas

It was one of those bad days.

Kitty never knew how they began.

Everything was

going wrong.

Dad said Kitty must have

got out of bed the wrong side.

She didn't want to do anything, and she

lost things, and nothing seemed fair.

Mum and Dad took no notice.

'Why aren't they worrying about me?'

she asked her brother Dan.

Dan said, 'They're in a good mood – but

you wouldn't understand that, Kitty.'

'Why not?' asked Kitty.

Dan laughed and said, 'Because you

don't know what a good mood is!'

He stuck his tongue out

at her and ran away.

Kitty had been cross before but now she

was very, very cross.

She chased her

brother down

the stairs . . .

. . . and out of the kitchen . . .

. . . and along the hall.

But he was too quick for her,

and slipped out through the front door.

Kitty stomped into the living room,
slamming the door behind her. And that
was when it started.

She slammed the door so hard it made

the room shake . . .

. . . and Mum's lovely old

jug on the table fell over

and broke into three pieces.

Worse than that, it fell
against Sandy's cage,
which was right at the
edge of the table.

The door flew open, and the terrified

hamster scuttled out across the carpet.

15

Kitty dived down to catch her.

But Sandy slipped

through her hands like

a bar of

wet soap.

Oops!

Sandy ran fast and

Kitty chased her,

knocking over ornaments

and photographs . . .

. . . and the wastepaper basket which

scattered rubbish all over the floor.

Kitty got on her hands and knees and

saw Sandy disappear behind the sofa.

18

Kitty knew she had to catch Sandy before she went down the hole in the skirting board and was lost forever! Quickly, she pulled off all the cushions.

Then she piled them at one end of the

sofa so Sandy couldn't get out.

Then, puffing and blowing, she pulled

the sofa away from the wall.

But the sofa knocked over the lamp . . .

. . . which knocked over a vase of flowers . . .

. . . and all the water poured

over the rug.

Suddenly Kitty spotted Sandy. She made a last grab, and caught her tightly in her hand.

She put Sandy safely back in her
cage and closed the door.

Then Kitty looked around and saw what she had done. There was stuff all over the place, and a wet patch on the rug.

It was terrible!

Two minutes later she went into the

kitchen smiling sweetly.

Mum handed Kitty a drink

and a chocolate biscuit.

'When we've had a drink, we're going to put some plants in the garden. Want to help, Kitty?' Mum said.

Kitty nodded and said, 'Oh, Mum, I'd love to.' Now Kitty hated gardening and Mum and Dad knew that. They gave each other a funny look.

Kitty knew she had to tell them what had happened in the living room, but she didn't know how to begin. So she said, 'I think you're the best parents in the world.'

Her mum and dad gave each other another funny look.

At last Kitty blurted out: 'If I tell you something, do you promise you won't be cross?' Her mum and dad promised.

Yes, Kitty.

Slowly, Kitty led them to the living room.

At the door she stopped.

'Sandy escaped, and I made a bit of a

mess in the living room trying to catch

her,' said Kitty.

Mum and Dad laughed.

Just a very little mess.

They opened the living room door.

Kitty stood well back.

Mum's face changed.

Kitty went backwards down the hall.

'Come here, Kitty!' Dad called. 'Do you call this a little mess!'

'How could you let this happen?' asked

Mum. She sounded really upset.

'But you promised you wouldn't be cross,' said Kitty, almost in tears.

'OK, OK,' said Dad, 'but now it's your turn to promise us something.'

Kitty agreed.

'Right then,' said Dad, '*You tidy the room.*'

Kitty groaned.

Kitty knew she had to start tidying. But she gave Sandy a cross look.

It took a long time to put everything in order. It was very hard work. Dan came to help, and tried to glue Mum's jug.

It looks a bit funny, Dan.

It's the best I can do, Kit.

At last the room looked better.

And Kitty found out that when
you tidy up, you sometimes come across
things you thought you'd lost.

Kitty ran into the garden to show Mum
and Dad the plaster model kit she'd got
for her birthday.

'Look – now I'm going to make you a
lovely present, Mum – to make up for
what I did to the living room,' she said.

Mum smiled. 'Oh, Kit – does that mean

you're going to make another mess?'

'I'll try not to,' Kitty said,

'but if I do . . .'

OH NO!

'Promise you won't be cross!'